The Queen and the Cats

A Story of Saint Helena

Written by
Calee M. Lee

Illustrated by
Turbo Qualls

Why are the people so tall?

I tried to see the queen. My sister, Mary, said she had a crown as tall as a donkey's ears. My brother, Peter, said she came in a ship larger than our house. Larger than Yiayia's house on top of our house.

But I still couldn't see.

Everyone was crowded onto the dock and into the wharf and all the way up to the center of the village. I tried to slip, slide or slink into any open space, but there was no getting through the crowd. The queen, the royal empress of the whole world had come to our little island and I wasn't going to get a glimpse.

There was just one more thing to try. I ran as fast as I could up the cobblestone hill, using my fingers to climb up the rocks when it got steep. I zipped through Irini's courtyard, and flew past the village oven we shared with our neighbors.

One more turn down a narrow street and there she was. Queen Helena was talking to Father George in front of the church. As the queen moved closer to the doors, the crowd drew back. I had my opening.

I couldn't hear what the priest said, but everyone heard her shout, "This will never do!"

She turned away from the abandoned church building and just when she had the same look Mama uses when we're in "first, middle and last name" trouble, Queen Helena saw me. When Mama gets that look, I usually run. But there were too many people. I wasn't going anywhere.

Just when I thought the queen would start throwing things, her eyes got very cold and she said in a soft, soft voice. "Little girl, come here."

Was I in trouble? She held out her hand. I froze. "Come here." I closed my eyes, reached out for her long soft fingers.

Yank! She pulled me so hard, I tumbled into her legs. The crowd—all of the people in my town, all of the people in my family—gasped. I knew what was coming now. Little girls don't bang into the Queen without having to spend their whole lives doing something horrible.

"You're safe now, little one." The queen bent down and ran her smooth fingers down my cheek. Then she pointed.

That teensy sliver of space I had just used for standing on was now home to a sandy-colored viper. The poisonous snake hissed in our direction and the crowd clambered to get a safe distance away.

The queen spoke and her voice echoed through the village, "Is it true that snakes like this one have taken over all of the churches of Cyprus?"

People nodded, murmured, kicked the ground because they knew it was true.

She continued, "I have brought you the greatest of treasures, but is there nowhere safe?"

The queen made a quick motion and one of her attendants laid a carefully wrapped parcel in her arm. "Would you like to see?" she asked me and I nodded, still thankful I wasn't being carted off in chains.

What? This was a treasure? Yet, this time when a murmur spread through the crowd, everyone started to bow.

I looked out over the people I saw every day. There was my mother, with her forehead resting on the street. It didn't make any sense.

I turned to the queen who was turning out to be the most confusing person I had ever met. I've never been very good at whispering so I just asked, "Your Majesty... Empress... my queen?" Gulp. This was harder than I thought. "Why is everyone bowing to a piece of wood?"

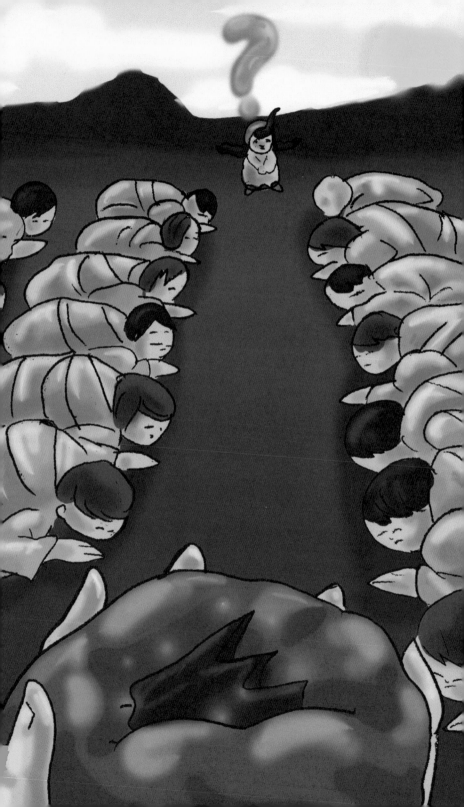

The queen bent down so I could see her eyes. I knew I didn't have to be scared but I still was.

"My dear child," she told me, "This is a piece of the True Cross. The cross where our Lord, Jesus Christ, died and defeated death. It is a very holy thing. Would you like to kiss it?"

I nodded and made the sign of the cross the way my mother taught me. Forehead, belly, shoulder, shoulder. She smiled then I smiled and kissed the sanded wood. It smelled like orange blossoms in the spring. It smelled like heaven.

Queen Helena raised the piece of the cross above her head. "I come from the holy land and have brought you a piece of the True Cross, that you and your families and all who come to live in this place may be blessed.

A small cheer rose up, then grew into a roar until I thought the stones of the church might topple from all our shouting.

As our cries died down, Queen Helena asked the priest, "You say that snakes have made this church unsafe, and I believe you. Is there anywhere on Cyprus where people can come and pray without worrying about their children's lives?"

Poor Father George. He had to answer no.

The queen was not used to being told "No," but there was nothing to be done. Snakes had made their nests in all of the churches and monasteries of Cyprus. Even though we wanted to worship God and venerate the holy cross, the snakes had deadly poison. It simply wasn't safe to go to church anymore.

All throughout her visit, Queen Helena fretted over the snake problem.

Finally, the night before her great ship was scheduled to leave; there was a special service at the church. For three days, my brother, Peter, and all of his friends had been standing guard, chasing all of the snakes away from the church with sticks dipped in oil and lit on fire.

When the time came, our whole village crowded inside the church. The bishop placed the holy cross in a special case and everyone had a chance to venerate it.

The next morning, Queen Helena, smiled when she saw me packed in between her chests and trunks and packages.

"Will you promise that you will take care of your church's great treasure for me?" she asked.

I nodded but then wondered, "What if my mother won't let me go near the Cross? What if it's not safe?"

Do you want to know a secret?" The queen's eyes twinkled. "I'm going to send you some special helpers. I don't think I will be able to return to Cyprus, but watch for my ship in the spring."

With that, the elegant lady gathered her skirts and took a big step onto the deck of the ship. She waved to the crowd and set sail.

Every day, I ran to the big rock at the tip of the harbor and looked across the wide, blue sea. Most mornings, I just saw a couple of birds fighting over fishing rights. But one day—just before Easter—there was a ship!

I was the first person to greet the royal vessel and I held my breath as I waited for the lovely queen to step out of her cabin.

The sailors tied the ship to the dock and began offloading their gear. "Little miss?" I turned at the captain's voice. "Her majesty couldn't make the journey, but she has sent a gift for you. Would you like to come aboard?"

We climbed deep into the hold of the ship. The captain said, "My lady mentioned you had a snake problem. I think this might clear it up."

He flung open the door.

Cats!

Black cats.

Grey cats.

Striped cats.

Orange cats.

White cats.

Lots and lots of cats!

Did you know that snake meat is very tasty if you are a cat?

Queen Helena's cats made
their homes in the churches and
monasteries of Cyprus, chasing away
the snakes and making it safe for us all
to come and pray.

Historical Note

Empress Helena of Constantinople journeyed to the Holy Land in the year 326 in search of the Holy Cross. When she reached Jerusalem, she supervised the excavation of the land where Jesus had been buried. When three crosses were discovered, a woman who was very sick was brought and began to touch the crosses. After touching the first two, nothing happened, but when she touched the third, she was miraculously healed. Saint Helena declared the cross that the woman had touched to be the True Cross. She brought back many of the holy treasures she found to her son, Constantine, the Emperor of Constantinople, but left several on the island of Cyprus where she spent some time. Today, every monastery is home not only to monks, but to cats, sometimes by the hundreds. Saint Helena is credited with sending the furry guardians to protect the faithful people from the poisonous snakes which had made the churches unsafe. Her feast day is celebrated on May 21st.

A piece of the Cross on display in Cyprus

Troparian to Saint Helena

The Empress Helena, mother of Constantine,
Was with us before
she sought the Cross in Jerusalem.
Thus, becoming like unto the apostles,
She calls us also to honor the Cross,
For in this sign, the standard of victory
over the enemy.
We are granted salvation and resurrection
And the triumph of the Heavenly Jerusalem.
Wherefore, O holy Helena, pray to Christ our
God that our souls may be saved

--To Nene.
Love, Nouna Calee

--To my family and especially my loving wife.
Love, Turbo

About the Author

Calee M. Lee visited the island of Cyprus for holy week in 2009 and fell in love with the country's beautiful scenery and friendly cats. A graduate of New York University's Tisch School of the Arts, Calee has worked extensively as a freelance writer, editor and video producer. She attends Saint Paul's Greek Orthodox Church in Irvine, California with her husband and two children.
She blogs at http://CaleeMLee.com

About the Illustrator

Turbo Qualls is an accomplished artist and illustrator in the Southern California area. Along with his wife and four children, Turbo attends St. Barnabas Orthodox Church in Costa Mesa, California.

Text © 2011 by Calee M. Lee
Illustrations © 2011 by Turbo Qualls
All rights reserved. First Edition
Published in the United States by Xist Publishing
www.xistpublishing.com
PO Box 61593 Irvine, CA 92602

ISBN-10: 0983842809 / ISBN-13: 978-0-9838428-0-4 (Xist Publishing)

Library of Congress Control Number: 2011936255

Printed in Great Britain
by Amazon